BILLY IS A BIG BOY

Are you a big boy too?

Written by

Don Hoffman

Illustrated by

Todd Dakins

Story and Text by Don Hoffman
Illustrated by Todd Dakins

Text and Illustrations Copyright © 2016, Don Hoffman

www.billyisabigboy.com • www.peekaboopublishing.com

Peek-A-Boo Publishing
Part of the Peek-A-Boo Publishing Group

Second Edition 2016 • Printed by Shenzhen TianHong Printing Co., Ltd. in Shenzhen, China

ISBN: 978-1-943154-25-8 (Hardback)
ISBN: 978-1-943154-02-9 (Paperback)
ISBN: 978-1-943154-39-5 (eBook)
ISBN: 978-1-943154-38-8 (PDF)
ISBN: 978-1-943154-40-1 (Mobi Pocket)

10 9 8 7 6 5 4 3 2

Today is Billy's birthday. Today it is true.

Today Billy is a big boy. Are you a big boy too?

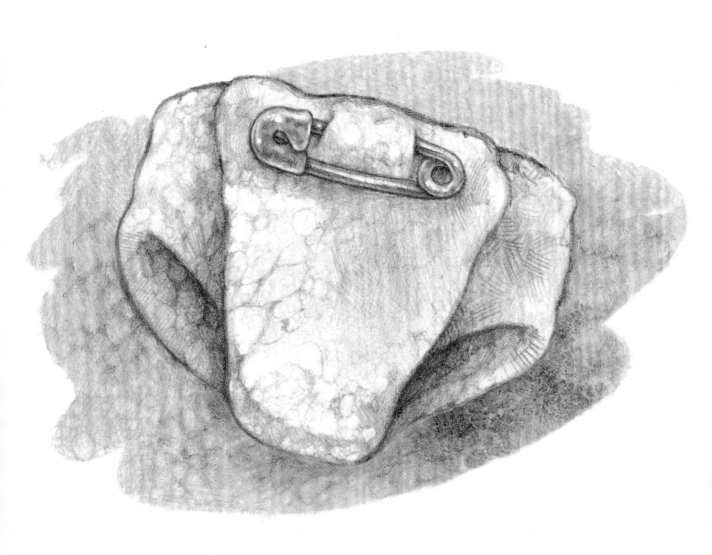

Billy used to wear diapers.

**Now he wears underpants. Billy is a big boy! How about you?
Do you wear underpants? Are you a big boy too?**

Billy used to have a bottle.

Now he uses a cup. Billy is a big boy! How about you?
Do you use a cup? Are you a big boy too?

Billy used to use a potty chair.

**Now he uses the toilet. Billy is a big boy! How about you?
Do you use the toilet? Are you a big boy too?**

Billy used to take baby baths.

Now he uses the bathtub. Billy is a big boy! How about you?
Do you use the bathtub? Are you a big boy too?

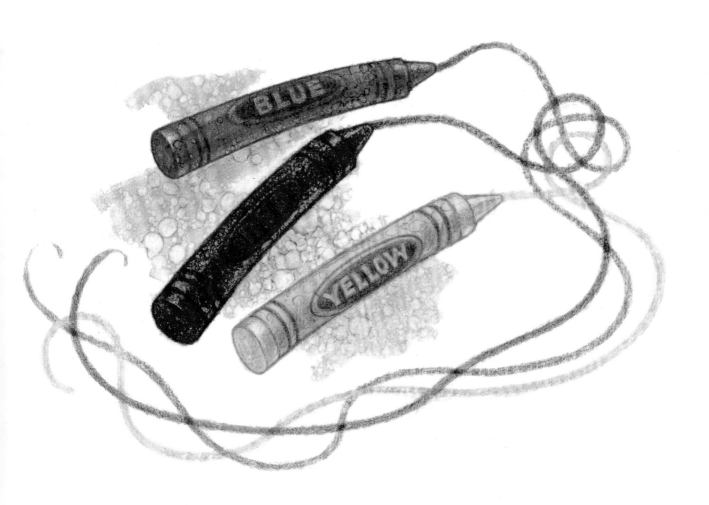

Billy used to draw only with crayons.

Now he can use a pencil too. Billy is a big boy! How about you?
Do you use a pencil? Are you a big boy too?

Billy used to talk baby talk.

Now he knows his ABCs. Billy is a big boy! How about you?
Do you know your ABCs? Are you a big boy too?

Billy used to use a high chair.

**Now he uses a booster seat. Billy is a big boy! How about you?
Do you use a booster seat? Are you a big boy too?**

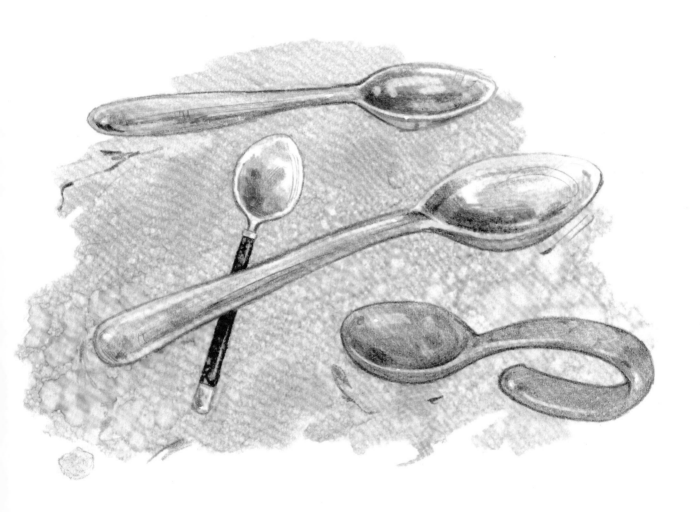

Billy used to eat with only a spoon.

Now he knows how to use a fork. Billy is a big boy! How about you? Do you know how to use a fork? Are you a big boy too?

**Just think! Soon Billy will ride a bicycle!
And so will you!**

And soon Billy will tie his own shoes.
And so will you!

 **BIG BOY**

"I did it!" Milestones for:

(my name)

I started wearing underpants
when I was ....

I started drinking from a cup
when I was ....

I started using the big potty
when I was ....

I started using the big bathtub
when I was ....

I started using a pencil
when I was ....

I could say my ABCs
when I was ----------------------------

I started sitting at the big table
when I was ----------------------------

I could use a fork
when I was ----------------------------

And guess what else I can do!

Place a picture
of yourself here.

Look who is a big boy too!